MARMALADE ATKINS' DREADFUL DEEDS

ANDREW DAVIES

Marmalade Atkins is not the worst girl in the world, though the people who know her think so. Her parents have more or less given up with her. Luckily they are rich and can afford to go on holiday or stay in another house when Marmalade becomes unbearable.

The only person that Marmalade respects is Rufus. Rufus is a donkey who wears an old straw hat and likes standing on people. One night Marmalade makes an important discovery about Rufus. He can talk. He likes Marmalade's style. No one has ever liked Marmalade's style before. He invites her to join him on his next night out – he's doing the star turn at El Poko Nightclub.

That's only the beginning ...

Cover shows Charlotte Coleman as Marmalade Atkins in the Thames TV series Educating Marmalade produced by Sue Birtwistle and directed by Colin Bucksey and John Stroud.

Marmalade Atkins' Dreadful Deeds

ANDREW DAVIES

Illustrated by John Laing

A Thames/Magnet Book

Also in Thames/Magnet

MARMALADE ATKINS IN SPACE

First published in Great Britain 1979 as *Marmalade and Rufus* by
Abelard-Schuman Ltd
A Member of the Blackie Group
Furnival House,
14–18 High Holborn London WC1V 6BX
Magnet paperback edition first published 1982 by
Methuen Children's Books Ltd
11 New Fetter Lane, London EC4P 4EE
in association with Thames Television International Ltd
149 Tottenham Court Road, London W1P 9LL
Reprinted 1982
Copyright © 1979 Andrew Davies
Illustrations copyright © John Laing
Printed in Great Britain by
Cox & Wyman Ltd, Reading

ISBN 0 423 00560 X

To Anna

Contents

Author's Note

At the beginning of a lot of books you find a note explaining that all the people and places are made up, and nothing to do with real life at all. This book is not quite like that; Rufus, Torchy, and Mad Gypsy Atkins are all real animals. And some of the things in this book really happened. Which ones those are, you will have to decide for yourself.

The only thing is to tell the truth from the start.

Marmalade Atkins was not a nice girl and Rufus was a pretty diabolical donkey.

There.

If you only like books about sweet little girls and gentle lovable donkeys, you had better pack it in now, and go and read some other book.

(The rest of this page is blank to give you time to make up your mind.)

A Bad Girl

Marmalade Atkins was not the worst girl in the world. People often said she was, but they were exaggerating. The people who said she was the worst girl in the world were: her mother, several teachers in the two schools Marmalade had been asked to leave, Miss Posy Fliss of the Lurnatrot Riding Stables, most of Marmalade's friends (they soon became enemies), and two or three psychologists, who had been called in to see what they could make of Marmalade's mind. Now these people did not really mean that she was the worst girl in the world. All they meant was that they had never met any worse girls themselves.

(By the way, if you think this is going to be one of those books in which the bad girl learns her lesson and becomes good and nice for ever after, you are wrong there too.)

Most of us feel like saying very rude things to people, and get the urge to do Bad Things. Marmalade Atkins was quite normal in this respect. What was different about her was that when she felt like saying rude things, she said them, and when she got the urge to do Bad Things, she did Bad Things. Here is an example:

One day Marmalade Atkins came downstairs and found a strange lady sitting on the edge of the sofa having coffee with Marmalade's mother. Marmalade realised at once that this was a nosy parker from the Council who had come to find out why Marmalade wasn't in school, or ask her silly questions, or see what she could make of Marmalade's mind. Marmalade had met several of these ladies before.

"Oh, Marmalade," said Marmalade's mother rather nervously, "this is Mrs Allgood. She's come to . . . she's . . ."

"I'm in one of the Helping Professions," said Mrs Allgood quickly and brightly, giving Marmalade her best Understanding Smile. "I've come to see if I can help you, Marmalade."

"I see you helped yourself to four chocolate biscuits," said Marmalade. Mrs Allgood went rather red, and Marmalade laughed at her until she went very red. This is going to be easy, thought Marmalade, sitting on Mrs Allgood's handbag and squashing it flat.

"That's Mrs Allgood's handbag," said Marmalade's mother, in a warning sort of voice.

"Blinking uncomfortable too," said Marmalade, shifting her bottom on the bag to get comfy. From inside the bag came the faint sound of breaking glass.

"Marmalade!" said Marmalade's mother.

Mrs Allgood put a gentle hand on Marmalade's mother's knee.

"It's all right, Mrs Atkins," she said gently. She

did her smile again for Marmalade.

"Could I have my bag please, dear?" she said. Marmalade got off the bag and handed it to Mrs Allgood, and Mrs Allgood looked at Marmalade's mother with smug triumph. "Now, dear," she said to Marmalade, "I'd like us to have a little talk. I haven't come to lecture you or tell you off. I want to hear Your Point of View."

She clasped her hands together, leaned forward, and gave Marmalade a long look of warm understanding (she was famous at the Council for her warm understanding looks). And Marmalade looked back.

She looks just like a fat old pig, thought Marmalade suddenly.

"You look just like a fat old pig!" said Marmalade to Mrs Allgood.

There was a short silence. Mrs Allgood went red again, and felt an unfamiliar feeling creeping up her chest. The feeling was hatred.

"Pig," said Marmalade, to keep the conversation going.

"I *beg* your pardon!" said Mrs Allgood unwisely.

"Deaf pig," said Marmalade.

"Marmalade. Out!" said Marmalade's mother sharply, and rather to Mrs Allgood's surprise, Marmalade got up and went upstairs.

"I expect you'd like to call it a day," said Marmalade's mother. "She doesn't seem to take to you."

"That girl," said Mrs Allgood between her

teeth, in a savage tone she had never heard herself use before, "that girl has *very serious problems*."

"At least," said Marmalade, coming downstairs, "I haven't got a problem like yours. Your problem is, you look like a pig!"

And she snatched Mrs Allgood's hat off her head, ran into the garden, and gave it to the goat, who ate part of it, and was later sick.

Mrs Allgood went back to the Council, and asked if she could retrain as a computer operator, and they said yes, and she did, and she lived happily ever after, thanks, you might say, to her meeting with Marmalade. She also cut down on the chocolate biscuits, so that she looked less like a pig, but not much less.

Several people came on visits like Mrs Allgood's, but I will not bore you with what Marmalade said and did. Enough to say that the Chief Educational Psychologist had to take a very long holiday in the Shetland Islands, the Senior Social Worker went off to start a chicken farm, and the School Attendance Officer joined the Army. All these people lived happily ever after, too, thanks, one might say, to meeting Marmalade Atkins.

Marmalade's mother found all these events rather a strain, and discovered that she enjoyed life a lot more when she and Marmalade were not in the same room, and even more than that when she and Marmalade were not in the same house. So she took to going out rather a lot, and

Marmalade found herself on her own a good deal of the time, which suited Marmalade fine.

But, you may be wondering, what about Marmalade's father? What about *Mr* Atkins? Has he run away to sea or something? She hasn't *killed him*, has she?

No, Marmalade's father was in very good health, and this was because he was usually away. Marmalade's father was very well off. He had three houses and five cars and two boats, and he had to work very long hours if he was to have any chance of using them all.

Also, he was absent-minded. He was so absent-minded that quite often he forgot which of his houses he was living in at the time, and went home to the wrong one, wondering vaguely why it was so quiet and where everyone was. On other occasions, remembering Marmalade, he went home to the wrong house on purpose. In fact, on the occasions when Marmalade did see her father, it was usually owing to a mistake on his part.

We have all read books about lovable absent-minded old professors, but I would not like you to think that Marmalade's father was like that. He was absent-minded of course, but he was neither lovable, nor old, nor a professor. He was a not very lovable youngish businessman, and I think the reason why he forgot not only his family's birthdays but even, sometimes, their names, was that he was not interested enough in such things to remember them.

As a matter of fact, it was because of Marmalade's father's absent-mindedness that Marmalade was called Marmalade. It happened like this:

Marmalade's father was particularly fond of satsumas, clementines, tangerines, ugli-fruit, and other unusual fruit of the orange type. His favourite of the lot was a clementine. He would often eat six or seven clementines for breakfast, he had clementine and chicory salad with his steak for lunch, he had clementine tarts for tea, and he even had a special clementine marmalade sent from a shop called Fortnum and Mason in London.

So when Marmalade was born, he thought that Clementine would be a good name for his little girl. His wife was so surprised that he had any ideas on the subject that she agreed at once.

Mr Atkins set off to see the Registrar of Births and Deaths, and managed to get there without once forgetting where he was going. When he walked into the office, he found that the Registrar was a lady, which took him rather by surprise, and perhaps that is why he forgot.

"What would you like to call the child?" said the Registrar, who was called Miss Allgood. (She was in fact Mrs Allgood's sister-in-law, but that is neither here nor there.)

Mr Atkins's mind went blank.

"Er . . . Marmalade," he said.

Miss Allgood smiled a special smile she had learnt from her sister-in-law.

"Are you quite sure, Mr Atkins?"

Mr Atkins thought. It didn't sound quite right, but he couldn't think what was wrong with it. Anyway, it wasn't as if it was going to be *his* name. *He* wasn't going to have to live with it for the next seventy years or so.

"Take your time, Mr Atkins," said the Registrar.

Mr Atkins took a deep breath.

"Quite sure," he said. "Marmalade Atkins it is."

When he got home from the Registrar's office he felt a bit peckish and went in the kitchen for a snack. He got out the marmalade. Halfway through the third slice of bread and marmalade he looked at the label.

FINEST CLEMENTINE MARMALADE
specially prepared and
blended by
FORTNUM AND MASON

Oh, said Marmalade's father to himself. Oh, dear. And then: Oh, well. And he spread himself a fourth slice.

And that was how Marmalade Atkins came by her name.

Marmalade Atkins, and Mrs Atkins, and Mr Atkins when he remembered to come home, lived on a farm. But they were not farmers, and it was not a proper farm. It consisted of a very pretty farmhouse, where the family lived, some very

15

pretty sheds and stables, where the animals lived, and a big barn where Mr Atkins threw parties for rich Arabs and sold them things. There were also an orchard and two fields. Mr Atkins had sold all the other fields to real farmers who rode up and down them in tractors and combine harvesters complaining about the weather.

It was the sort of farm that had one of everything. There was a sheep called Dolores, who had a very boring personality and was a disappointment to everyone, a goat called Garth, who was moody and ate hats, a cow called Elsie, who was by no means as mild as she looked; there was the Hen with No Name, and there was a Free Range Piglet called Rover, who spent most of his time running round in circles trying to catch his tail. Sometimes in the evenings, after he had had a hard day with the Arabs, Mr Atkins would come home, change into a tweed hat and leggings, and lean on a gate, saying "Ar. This be the loife" to himself over and over again. He had a real farmer's knobbly stick, too, with which he used to poke Rover the Free Range Piglet, saying "Ar. Foine bit o' bacon, that be" until one evening when Rover turned nasty and bit Mr Atkins in the leg. After that Mr Atkins left the pig-poking out of his nightly routine, and chewed a piece of straw instead.

Marmalade's mother, who had to do most of the feeding and milking and mucking out and other disgusting farmyard tasks, would become so furious at the sight of her husband leaning on the

16

gate saying "Ar" for hours on end that she would stamp upstairs, pick up the telephone and order long strings of expensive items such as fur coats, French perfume, and liqueur chocolates on Mr Atkins's account at Harrods of Knightsbridge.

But the three most important animals on the farm lived together in a big stable in the larger of the two fields. And their names were Gypsy, Torchy, and Rufus.

Gypsy was a medium-sized brown horse with a friendly face and huge gentle brown eyes. He was very mild-mannered (in Marmalade's opinion he was a big softy) and he would let Torchy and Rufus push him around and eat his hay without complaint. He liked to nuzzle people and have his head scratched, and if you tickled his lower lip he would raise his head and flash you a huge toothy grin. In fact Gypsy was everyone's idea of the perfect horse. Until anyone got on his back, that is.

When anyone got on his back, Gypsy got the Red Mist. His idea of a good time was to run very fast indeed in a straight line until he came to something in the way, such as a gate or a hedge or a wall. These obstructions always seemed to come as a complete surprise to Gypsy. Sometimes he would jump the obstacle, sometimes he would stop dead, and sometimes he would run straight into it at full speed. If you were on his back, the result was more or less the same. You would fall off, and Gypsy would trot quietly up to you and nuzzle you affectionately. Few people rode Gypsy twice.

Torchy was a fat white pony who went round with a secret smile on his face. He was a very nice pony to ride if you didn't mind stopping every few yards for him to have a snack. The other thing he liked to do was roll on his back kicking his legs in the air, and most people found it best to dismount while he was doing this.

And then there was Rufus. Rufus had come with the farm and nobody knew how old he was. He wore an old straw hat that didn't suit him, but nobody had ever dared to take it off, because although Rufus usually looked half asleep, there was a certain look about his half-shut eyes that warned you not to take liberties with Rufus or his hat.

After his hat, the next thing you noticed about Rufus was his coat, which was rough and thick, and several kinds of red in colour. There were sandy tufts, and gingery tufts, and carroty whorls, and pinkish stubble. His coat was of several different lengths, and grew in several different directions, and he looked as if he had just paid a visit to a drunken barber's. Despite all this, he seemed a nice old thing, and people who didn't know him would cry out: "Oh, what a sweet little donkey! Isn't he a love!" and people who did know him would clear their throats and change the subject, and Rufus himself would throw back his head and let out a sarcastic "Hee-*haw*!" in his very loud and vulgar voice, and if you looked into his sleepy old eyes you could see his crafty old brain ticking over, working out something bad to do.

Because Rufus was a pretty diabolical donkey.

Rufus liked to give people surprises. One way of doing this was to come up behind them and give them a very gentle nudge with his nose. Usually they would stroke his muzzle saying "What a sweet old thing!" Then he would give them another nudge, a bit harder, then a very hard nudge indeed. After about three nudges, most people fell down, and Rufus would stand on them. Donkeys look small, but they weigh at least twice as much as your fattest auntie, and it is no joke being stood on by a donkey like Rufus.

Marmalade's mother would try to smooth the situation over by whacking him with a twig and saying "Don't be a bore, Rufus!" or "It's only his way of showing he likes you!" but people who were stood on by Rufus wished he could show his affection in some other way; and those who looked up into his wickedly gleaming eyes thought, but didn't like to say, that Marmalade's mother was quite wrong and that Rufus did not in fact like them at all.

And in this they were usually right.

Marmalade, Rufus
and Cherith Ponsonby

The day on which the Strange Events began was
the day Cherith Ponsonby and her mother came
to visit the Atkinses. Cherith Ponsonby was the
head girl of the school which Marmalade Atkins
had most recently been asked to leave. Marmalade Atkins disliked Cherith Ponsonby because
she was a goody-goody, because she was a posh
snob, because she was head girl, because she was a
big softy, and because she had a name like a lisp.
Cherith Ponsonby disliked Marmalade Atkins because everyone else did and it was the Done
Thing.

So while the two mothers drank their coffee and
talked about Harrods, and Fortnum and Mason,
and the new by-pass, and how awful Mr Atkins
and Mr Ponsonby were, Marmalade Atkins and
Cherith Ponsonby sat at opposite ends of the room
and glared at each other. After rabbiting on for
about four whole hours on the topics mentioned
above, Mrs Atkins and Mrs Ponsonby switched to
sherry, and Mrs Ponsonby gave a meaning glance
at the two girls, which was a signal that it was
time to go into Detail about the ways in which Mr
Atkins and Mr Ponsonby were awful.

"Wouldn't you like to take Cherith outside to
play?" said Marmalade's mother.

"Not a lot," said Marmalade. She looked across at Cherith Ponsonby. Cherith Ponsonby was wearing a new glossy hard riding hat, a new herringbone tweed hacking jacket, new Bedford Cord jodhpurs, and brand new handmade riding boots of a strikingly horrible yellow colour.

"What d'you want to do, play football?" said Marmalade.

"I think she'd like to ride, dear," said Cherith Ponsonby's mother.

"Grr," said Marmalade, and stomped off to get her boots.

"I used to have a pair of boots like that," said Cherith as they crossed the yard, "but I gave them away."

Marmalade said nothing.

"The nuns still talk about you at school," said Cherith as they went into the paddock.

Marmalade did not reply.

"I heard them the other day," said Cherith. "Sister Purification was telling Sister Conception that you were the most revolting little creature she had ever met in her whole life."

"Was she?" said Marmalade. "Here's Rufus."

Rufus walked sleepily across the paddock to the two girls. Then he stopped, staring at Cherith's yellow boots as if they were some sort of deliberate insult.

"D'you like his hat?" said Marmalade.

"I think he looks quite ridiculous," said Cherith.

Rufus looked at Cherith thoughtfully, and

Marmalade waited eagerly for him to give her one of his extra hard nudges, knock her down, and stand on her. But to Marmalade's intense disappointment he stayed where he was, chewing sleepily.

"What a boring donkey," said Cherith.

Marmalade concentrated hard on the exact spot on Cherith's jodhpurs where she planned to plant her boot, but at the last moment Cherith turned away.

"Can I ride Torchy now?" she said.

"Try Gypsy," said Marmalade hopefully. Perhaps Gypsy would be in the mood for jumping the goat or running into the barn wall.

"No, I want Torchy," said Cherith. "I've heard about what Gypsy does."

So Torchy it had to be. Marmalade tried everything. She left things undone, she put the stirrups at different lengths, she did the girths up loose in the hope that Cherith would slide down the side till she was hanging underneath the little pony's fat belly, but Cherith spotted the lot, and trotted away with a toss of her head.

Marmalade had to admit that she was a good rider. She was making Torchy go straight instead of sideways, and every time he tried to stop for a snack she made him go on. Rufus came and stood by Marmalade and Marmalade leaned against him grumpily.

"Rufus, you have let me down," said Marmalade. "You're supposed to be a diabolical donkey, and you have let that softy insult you and get away with it."

Rufus turned his sleepy old head, and for a split second Marmalade was sure that she saw him wink his left eye. Then, moving at a speed that amazed her, he was off. He careered in a crazy zigzag all round the field, swinging his head in a wild arc and getting up speed all the time, then he headed straight for Torchy and Cherith. Poor Torchy was scared out of his wits. He reared, bucked, leapt straight up in the air, and then bolted. Cherith Ponsonby flew into the air and landed in a thistle patch. One of her new yellow boots came off. The goat ate part of it and was sick almost immediately.

Marmalade followed Rufus round to the front yard, and watched him back slowly and carefully up to Mrs Ponsonby's Mercedes and give it a good kicking. Mrs Ponsonby's Mercedes was a new car, and very strongly built, but it was no match for an expert like Rufus. He gave it a truly diabolical kicking and it was never the same again. Mrs Ponsonby came over faint, and Cherith Ponsonby had hysterics, and Marmalade Atkins laughed so much that her mother sent her to her room for the rest of the day, and Rufus trotted back to join the horses, sleepy and content after his morning's work.

In the evening, when she had been let out, Marmalade Atkins came downstairs and walked across the yard. She climbed over the gate on which her father was leaning, muttering to himself about this being the life, ar, ar, and she walked down to the stable. It was dark and peaceful in the stable. Gypsy, Torchy and Rufus were standing in a row quietly munching their hay. Marmalade sat on a box and watched Rufus contentedly, thinking how much she liked and admired his attitude to life. After a long while she said softly: "Rufus, I take it back, what I said. You were good this morning. You were. You were diabolically good."

Rufus turned his scruffy old head and looked at her.

"You're a bit of a mean 'un yourself," he said.

Marmalade held her breath. Was she awake or dreaming? Had Rufus really spoken? Was she going mad? The moment seemed to go on for ever: the quiet dark stable, the steady slow munching of Gypsy and Torchy, Marmalade's heart thumping away under her teeshirt, and her breath caught, trapped in her chest as she waited to see if Rufus would speak again.

But he didn't speak. He stared at her for a long moment, then he jerked his scruffy old head

towards the farm, and the next thing Marmalade knew was that she was running as fast as she could go across the paddock, scrambling over the gate, thudding across the yard, grabbing at the kitchen door, and running upstairs; where, to her mother's surprise, she washed, cleaned her teeth, and went straight to bed and turned the light out.

Downstairs, Marmalade's mother turned to Marmalade's father as he sat in his tweed hat trying to light a clay pipe.

"I don't like it," she said. "That girl is behaving more strangely every day. *I* don't know where she gets it from. *My* family have always been quite normal."

She glared at her husband accusingly.

Mr Atkins threw a used match into the grate, where it lay in a heap with thirty-seven other used matches. He often took a whole box to get his pipe lit.

"Ar," he said finally. "Nowt so queer as folk."

"Oh, really, Humphrey, do you *have* to be so impossible?" shouted Marmalade's mother.

"Ar," said Marmalade's father. He really enjoyed saying "Ar" and he didn't give two hoots one way or another about being impossible. In his opinion Marmalade's mother was just as impossible as he was, anyway.

"If you think," said Marmalade's mother, "that I am going to spend the evening of this dreadful day sitting about listening to you going Ar, Ar, Ar, you have got another think coming. I am going out to play bridge with the Paget-

Brownes." And she leapt up, flung her fur coat dramatically round her shoulders, slammed out of the farmhouse, got into her Jaguar, and drove away.

"Ar," said Marmalade's father to himself. "Ar. Ar."

After a while he became tired of saying "Ar" and started to feel bored and lonely. He went upstairs, looked in at Marmalade, who was fast asleep, changed into a smart suit, went out to his Rolls Royce, and drove to the Dorchester Hotel in London where he played poker with some Arabs he knew and lost his gold cuff-links.

In doing this, they had left Marmalade alone in the house, which was unwise as well as being illegal.

Marmalade Atkins
and the Night Conversation

Suddenly Marmalade was awake. She sat straight up in bed and listened. Someone was moving about downstairs. It wasn't her mother, whose high heels echoed on the oak floors like whip-cracks. It wasn't her father, who slouched. It was someone who wore very heavy boots, with metal caps or something like that on, and this someone was moving with a tread so heavy that the walls vibrated. It must be a very big burglar.

Now most girls would be terrified if they heard this sort of thing. They would huddle down under the bedclothes and tell themselves they were dreaming, they would shiver and shake, they would hug their teddies. But Marmalade, as we have seen, was not like most girls. She had often wished she could meet a burglar and ask him about his life, which must be an exciting and interesting one, she thought. In fact she had sometimes thought that she would like to be a burglar when she grew up.

Very quietly Marmalade Atkins slipped out of bed and put her slippers on. It was important not to disturb the burglar, or he might run off without taking anything. There were several things that Marmalade wanted burgled. Her Brownie uniform was one of them. And there were several china models of dancers belonging to her mother on the mantelpiece; their soppy expressions had got on Marmalade's wick for years, but perhaps a burglar would think them worth taking. And if he had a van, she thought eagerly, he might agree to take the Encyclopaedia Britannica, Every Child's Passport to Success. Horrible great lurking thing. Marmalade tiptoed to the door and listened.

The burglar seemed to have stopped moving around. And very faintly Marmalade could hear the sound of the television. She was impressed. This must be a very cool burglar, taking a rest to watch telly before getting on with his work. If he was nicely settled, now would be the time to go down and introduce herself.

She tiptoed down the stairs and across the hall. The living room door was open a tiny crack. Marmalade Atkins put her eye to the crack. Yes, the telly was on. Green, black, red, flashes of brown. Horses. It must be the Horse of the Year Show. And sitting watching it, slumped in the middle of the sofa, was the burglar.

Most of the burglar was hidden by the high back of the sofa, but the bits that Marmalade could see looked very strange indeed. The burglar seemed to be wearing a flat check cap very like one that Marmalade's father had, and underneath the cap some sort of reddish woolly thing like a Balaclava helmet. But it wasn't an ordinary Balaclava helmet. It had ears. Long ears. Long ears that stuck up straight in the air. Like a donkey's ears.

Marmalade paused and held her breath, and over the sound of the television she heard a wheezy creaking sound, halfway between a chuckle and someone sitting on a set of bagpipes. Then a hoarse voice, like a voice that hadn't been used for years, said:

"Daft 'oss."

Marmalade opened the door wide and stepped in.

The burglar turned.

"Evenin', Marmalade Atkins," said the burglar.

It was Rufus.

Rufus did not seem in the least shy about being caught lolling on the sofa. He seemed perfectly at home. He nodded amiably at Marmalade and gestured with his hoof at the bag of apples by his side. Marmalade took one without thinking, and started eating it.

"That's my girl," said Rufus, and turned back to the television. Marmalade decided to assert herself.

"Now look here, Rufus," she said. "I'm not your girl, you're my donkey! Who d'you think you are, coming in here and rolling your great hairy body about on our sofa, and eating our apples and watching our television, and wearing my father's hat—you look *daft* in it—and *talking*, donkeys don't *talk*, don't you *know* that, and generally carrying on as if you own the place. It simply won't do. What's your game?"

Rufus spat an apple pip into the fire.

"Do own the place. Cheeky monkey."

Marmalade was enraged. She didn't seem to be impressing him at all. He had even turned back to watch the telly.

"Rufus!" she shouted.

Rufus did his wheezy chuckle again.

"Look at them daft horses," he said. "They haven't got the sense they was born with."

Marmalade began to feel that she was on the losing side in this conversation, which was an unusual feeling for her.

"What d'you mean, you own the place?" she said crossly. "My father paid a lot of money for it."

"Don't mean a thing to me, Marmalade," said Rufus. "I was here before he was."

"Right! Right!" shouted Marmalade. "You came with the farm, you did, he bought you with it, he bought you for me, so you're my donkey, see? Get it? *Eh*?"

Rufus turned his head slowly and looked at Marmalade as she stood there in her nightie all red in the face and stamping her foot. Marmalade began to feel rather silly, and stopped stamping.

"I'm me own donkey," he said. "Always was, always will be."

Marmalade couldn't find an answer to that one, though she racked her brains till they hurt. She thought she might think better if she sat down, so she sat on a little stool by Rufus's feet, and looked up at him. He looked very big and old and clever, and she felt weak and small.

"What about all this talking then?" she said grumpily. "How long have you been able to talk?"

"Always," said Rufus. "Nothing to it."

"Ho," said Marmalade Atkins craftily. "Why haven't you done any talking before then?"

"Never saw the need of it," said Rufus. "People round here are such a lot of fools, I wouldn't waste me breath on them."

Marmalade thought about this for a minute or two. And then she said in a small and thoughtful voice:

"But you've started to talk to me. Why did you want to talk to me?"

For the first time Rufus paused before answering. He shifted his huge gingery bulk this way and that on the sofa, leaving several coarse ginger hairs and a damp muddy stain on the flowered chintz. It was almost as if he was embarrassed.

"Like your style," he said grudgingly. "Like the way you handle yourself."

Marmalade had stopped feeling angry. Instead she was feeling very strange. Rufus liked her style, whatever that meant. He didn't want to talk to her mother, however smart and good at bridge she was, and he didn't want to talk to her father, however rich and absent-minded he was, and he clearly didn't want to talk to big softy Cherith Ponsonby, however goody-goody she was. He wanted to talk to Marmalade Atkins, because he liked her style. Nobody had ever liked Marmalade's style before, whatever that meant, and it felt very good to know that Rufus did.

But there must be a catch in it somewhere. Life, Marmalade knew, was like that. She thought for a minute or two and then decided she knew what it was.

"Listen, Rufus," she said. "You're not one of those talking animals who come up to bad children in fairy stories and make them feel all soft and soppy inside so that they turn into big softies and goody-goodies like Cherith Ponsonby? You're not one of those animals, are you, because if you are, *bad luck*!"

"No, Marmalade Atkins," said Rufus, "I'm not one of them sort of animals at all."

Marmalade did some more thinking.

"What sort of animal are you then?" she said.

"I'm an animal to be reckoned with," said Rufus proudly.

"I knew that," said Marmalade.

"Right then," said Rufus. He turned back to the television as if the conversation was over. Marmalade waited a long time but nothing else happened. She was getting used to sitting in the living room late at night with a talking donkey in a checked cap. She hoped that this was not all there was going to be to it. She tried to be patient and wait for the next thing, but the next thing seemed a long time coming and she was not used to being patient. In the end she had to say something.

"What's it like?" she said.

"What's what like?" said Rufus irritably. The

Horses of the Year were having a jump-off and he
seemed to be getting involved despite himself.

"Being a donkey," said Marmalade.

"Terrible," said Rufus briefly.

"Why?" said Marmalade.

Rufus turned wearily away from the telly and
fixed his sleepy eyes on her.

"Well," he said, "How would you like folks to
call you a sweet little thing, and put silly hats on
you, and try to get on your back and ride round

34

on you, and put you in a cold old stable with a couple of daft young ponies without ever once asking if you wouldn't rather have a bed like what they've got? Eh?"

"I wouldn't like it at all," said Marmalade. "I wouldn't put up with it."

"Neither do I," said Rufus. "I takes liberties. But plenty of donkeys don't."

On the television, a rider called Buster Creighton incurred four faults and was eliminated from the final round. Rufus gave a brief guffaw and turned back to Marmalade.

"Added to which," he said, "I'm an old donkey, I am. Know how long I been on this farm?"

"No," said Marmalade, walking into it.

"Donkey's years!" roared Rufus, falling about laughing.

There was a sound of splintering wood from inside the sofa and one of the arms fell sideways and sagged pathetically towards the floor.

"Oh dear, oh dear," said Rufus, not looking sorry at all. "Never mind. Not often I get a good laff."

Marmalade wondered who would get blamed for the broken sofa. She did not need to wonder long. It would be her, of course, unless she could spin a story about a bunch of Arabs coming looking for her father and overloading the sofa with their camels or something. Yes, no problem: she would think of a good story. Anything would seem more likely than the truth.

"No, to be serious," said Rufus, "the thing about being a donkey is you live so long. After the first ninety years or so, folk start getting on your wick. You feel like taking a few liberties and putting yourself about a bit."

"I've seen you at it," said Marmalade.

"What d'you think of it?" said Rufus.

"I like it," said Marmalade. "I like to take a few liberties myself."

"I've been watching you," said Rufus. "I reckon you and I could have a bit of fun together."

"What sort of fun?" said Marmalade Atkins.

"All sorts of fun," said Rufus. "Take that Buster Creighton, for one. He's had it coming to him for a bit. He wants pushing over and standing on, he does."

Marmalade stared at her donkey in admiration and awe.

"You mean you're going to knock Buster Creighton down and stand on him?"

"Course I am," said Rufus, "I'm going to give that Buster Creighton a right seeing to, no problem. No hurry. I can bide my time. Course, they'll hush it up, like when I pushed that Mark Philpotts in the manure heap. He's another right one for getting on horses' backs and making them jump over things. I can't abide that. Makes me want to knock 'em down and stand on 'em."

"And when you want to, you do," said Marmalade.

"Well, that's obvious," said Rufus. Marmalade

felt a deep surge of affection for Rufus. She had never met anyone who felt like she did before.

"Do you do anything else, or do you just knock people down and stand on them?" she said. "Not that I'm criticising, of course."

"That's not the half of what I gets up to," said Rufus mysteriously.

"What else do you get up to?" said Marmalade.

"Well," said Rufus. "I gets dressed up and I goes out . . . ."

"And?" said Marmalade.

"And I puts myself about a bit," said Rufus modestly.

"But *how*?" said Marmalade. She simply had to know.

"All sorts of ways," said Rufus vaguely. Marmalade felt let down, and Rufus seemed to sense it.

"Come and see for yourself if you like, one of these nights."

"Can I really?"

"Often felt like a bit of company," said Rufus.

"But how will I wake up?" said Marmalade.

"Oh, you'll wake up. I'll be down here. You sneak down the stairs like, and I'll be waiting for you, and then we'll go out, and by heck we'll put ourselves about a bit."

How Marmalade Atkins
Nearly Starved to Death

That was the last thing Marmalade Atkins remembered of the strange night conversation. The next thing she knew, she was lying awake in bed, it was morning, birds were singing outside the windows, and somewhere in the distance was the familiar sound of Rufus hee-hawing his morning greeting to the world.

How disappointing. How infuriatingly *feeble*. She must have dreamed the whole lot. The Horse of the Year Show, the checked cap, the talking donkey, everything. Why did dreams have to be so much more interesting than real life? And what a fool she had been to think it was all really true. No, Rufus was just an ordinary donkey. Diabolical, but just a donkey. Oh, well, back to normal. Grr.

In a thoroughly bad mood, Marmalade got out of bed, put her slippers on, and stamped down the stairs to breakfast. Her mother was sitting at the table looking at her very coldly. Now what? thought Marmalade grimly.

"Marmalade Atkins," said her mother. "I have a bone to pick with you."

"Oh," said Marmalade.

"Yes," said her mother.

"I want you to explain that disgusting mess in

the lounge."

Marmalade felt her heart give a thump.

"What mess?" she said, hoping against hope.

"You know very well what mess!" shouted her mother, suddenly losing her temper, and she grabbed Marmalade's arm, yanked her to her feet, and propelled her into the lounge.

"There! That mess!" she screamed, pointing at the sofa.

The sofa was covered in gingery hairs and damp muddy stains, and one arm sagged pathetically towards the floor. It was true! It had happened! It hadn't been a dream! Rufus had left his mark.

"I am waiting," said Marmalade's mother. "I want to know what on earth you were doing last night."

"It wasn't me," said Marmalade, before she had time to think. "It was Rufus."

She went cold inside. But she needn't have worried.

"Little liar," said her mother. "Come on. Tell me what you did."

"You can't pin that on me," said Marmalade. "I'm not strong enough to wreck a sofa. How could I have managed a thing like that, eh?"

"That," said her mother, "is what you are going to tell me. Or I shall call the police."

"Camels," said Marmalade.

"*What*?"

"It was the camels," said Marmalade. "Two of them. Dad went out, and a bit later some Arabs

39

came to call for him. They brought their camels with them. I told them not to bring the camels in, but the Chief Arab said the camel was a sacred beast where he came from, and where he laid his head, his camel laid his head too. So they came in with their camels, and laid their heads on the sofa, and so did the camels, but the camels were too heavy for the sofa, and it bust.''

She paused. Somehow the story didn't seem quite so convincing as she had hoped it would be.

Her mother didn't seem to like it very much either. She began to tremble all over, from head to foot, in such a rage that she could hardly speak. But she was a lady of great self-control, was Marmalade's mother, and after trembling with silent rage for seven and a half minutes, she was able to speak quite calmly to her daughter.

"Right," she said. "Very good. Excellent. If you wish to play silly games, that is your affair. But until you tell me the truth, you will have no breakfast, no lunch, no tea, and no supper.''

"But I have told you the truth," said Marmalade. She had, too; it was quite funny in a way, and she couldn't help smiling.

"Fine," said her mother. "Glad to see you are enjoying yourself. Let's see how you feel by the end of the day.''

"I'll steal my own food," said Marmalade.

"You most certainly will not," said her mother, locking the door of the kitchen.

"There's laws against starving your children," said Marmalade.

"There are laws against smashing people's sofas," said her mother, and swept upstairs to her bedroom, where she immediately got on the telephone to Harrods of Knightsbridge to ask them the name of their most expensive perfume, and the largest sized bottle in which it could be bought. Marmalade spent five minutes trying to pick the lock of the kitchen door, then gave up and went outside to find Rufus.

She found him standing in the middle of his field, absentmindedly chewing a bit of hay that was sticking out of the side of his mouth. He looked half asleep as usual, and very much like himself. It seemed impossible to believe that last night he had been watching television and rolling around smashing sofas. Marmalade fixed him with the cold stare she had learnt from her mother.

"Listen, Rufus," she said. "I've got a bone to pick with you."

Rufus didn't even look up.

"You got me into a lot of trouble last night. I'm to be starved to death on your account, you know."

Rufus made no reply.

"Rufus, I'm talking to you", said Marmalade, beginning to feel rather silly. "I know you can talk. Come on, what have you got to say for yourself?"

Rufus turned round slowly so that Marmalade found herself looking at a large scruffy ginger bottom.

"That's not very nice," said Marmalade.

"Where's your manners?"

Rufus suddenly gave a loud hoarse grunt, and launched himself into one of his crazy zigzag runs across the field, tossing his head from side to side and hee-hawing in the most ear-splitting way, giving Gypsy such a severe fright that he ran at full speed into the stable and forgot to stop when he was in there. Gypsy's head whacked straight into the wooden wall, splintering one of the planks. After a minute or two he came out, walking in a rather vague and dizzy fashion, and stared dopily at Rufus, who was by now in his original position in the middle of the field. Gypsy liked Rufus but he had never been able to get used to the hee-haw runs.

Marmalade decided to be patient. It was a difficult thing for her, but she was determined. Rufus was obviously not going to speak just when she wanted him to, and she would just have to wait until he was ready.

She followed him round all day. And to her annoyance he did absolutely nothing out of the ordinary. He spent most of the day standing still and staring into space, turning his bottom towards Marmalade whenever she approached. At lunch-time he led Torchy into a thick bramble patch, where Torchy got stuck as he always did, and Rufus strolled round to the stable and ate Torchy's lunch. Then he strolled back to the bramble patch and showed Torchy how to get out.

At half past two the postman's van came, and

Rufus trotted round amiably to see the postman. The postman gave him a lump of sugar, and Rufus nuzzled up to him and tried to bite the buttons off his uniform. As the postman was about to leave, Rufus walked up to his van in a humble inoffensive sort of way, and turned his backside to it. Marmalade held her breath.

But the postman was no fool, and besides that, he was in training for the Mad Driver of the Year competition. He slammed into reverse, backed smartly into Marmalade's mother's Jaguar, and zoomed off in a shower of rust and a tinkle of broken glass. Rufus strolled back to the field as if all this had nothing whatsoever to do with him.

Later on in the afternoon, Rufus's girlfriend Jenny, a donkey who belonged to the neighbouring farmer, came down to the fence and started calling to him. He ignored her for a bit, then trotted over to the fence, chose a weak bit, and kicked it down. He seemed to be able to do this without exerting himself at all. Jenny watched him with what looked to Marmalade like shy admiration as he shouldered his way calmly through the gap he had made and sauntered up to her. Marmalade was interested to see that he let Jenny play some rather silly games with him. Jenny was a young and rather flighty donkey, and she liked to run round Rufus in circles, bumping her bottom into him. He even let her give his ratty old tail a few gentle nips, which amazed Marmalade Atkins. Rufus's ratty old tail was a no-go territory for everyone in the normal way: to meddle with it spelt instant death.

After this, Rufus walked Jenny slowly back to her stable and went in it with her. Marmalade went as close as she dared to see if she could hear them talking, but so far as she could tell they didn't talk at all. Rufus stayed there till it was getting dark, then he walked back through the gap and went into his own stable and started pushing the horses around. He had not uttered a single word all day.

Marmalade stamped back into the house, feeling hungry and cross. Marmalade's mother looked up from her travel brochure.

"Ah," she said, "Marmalade. Have you decided to tell the truth yet?"

"I did," said Marmalade, "but you wouldn't believe me."

"Very well," said her mother. "Go to bed."

"You are a cruel woman," said Marmalade, "and if I starve to death you will have no one to blame for it but yourself."

She dragged herself up the stairs, feeling herself grow weaker with every step, and her mother picked up the telephone and booked herself a winter sports holiday in the most expensive hotel in Switzerland.

"No children, we regret," said the travel agent.

"That suits me fine," said Marmalade's mother.

Good-Time Rufus

Marmalade Atkins woke up in the middle of the night feeling very hungry indeed. Her first thought was that she had not starved to death after all, and in a way that was quite disappointing. On the other hand, she was awake now, and if she didn't do something about the hollow feeling in her stomach she would probably be too weak to move by morning. Perhaps her mother had forgotten to keep the kitchen locked all night. If so, she was going to regret it, because Marmalade Atkins felt like eating every scrap of food in the house. She leapt out of bed grinding her teeth and muttering about sausages to herself, and without quite knowing why she was doing it, she got her best jeans (the only ones without ink and grass stains) out of the wardrobe and pulled them on. She slipped down the stairs and tried the kitchen door. It opened!

But Marmalade Atkins had barely had time to cram down six cold sausages when she heard a muffled curse from the direction of the lounge. It didn't sound like an Atkins curse or an Arab curse. She hardly dared to hope, but it sounded like...

"That you, Marmalade Atkins? In here, quick," said a now familiar voice.

She opened the door of the lounge and went in. Rufus was standing in front of the mirror scowling at himself, with the muddy and crumpled ends of a black bow tie dangling loosely from his thick hairy neck.

"You any good with these things?" he said. He looked quite agitated.

"You don't want to wear a bow tie, do you?" said Marmalade.

"Case of having to," said Rufus. "Come on, you got hands, must be easy for you."

Marmalade was not very good at tying bow ties either, but after a struggle she managed to get it done. One side looked bigger than the other, and the whole thing was damp and smelly, but Rufus seemed content.

"Hm," he said, turning his head this way and that. "Have to do."

"I think you look daft in it," said Marmalade rudely. She had still not forgiven him for the previous night, or for refusing to speak to her all day.

But he didn't seem offended.

"That may be," he said. "But standards have to be kept up. Come on. Taxi's waiting."

"*What?*" said Marmalade.

"Taxi. Going out. Going to put ourselves about, like I said."

"But it's the middle of the *night*," said Marmalade.

"Can't help that," said Rufus. "You coming or not?"

"Of course I am," said Marmalade. "And stop being so bossy."

"Right, miss," said Rufus, and opening the latch with his teeth, led the way out.

In the middle of the yard stood a small grey shiny horsebox that Marmalade had never seen before. A little man with a foxy face and a pencil moustache got down from the driver's seat, raised his grey peaked cap, and opened the back door.

"Evenin' Perkins," said Rufus.

"Evenin' sir," said the little foxy man.

"This is Miss Marmalade Atkins," said Rufus rather grandly. "She will be accompanying us."

"Right, sir, I see," said Perkins. "Glad to have you with us, miss."

"You can sit up front with Perkins if you like," said Rufus, "but he will rabbit on about football, never known such a boring man. Dreadful bore, aren't you Perkins?"

"Certainly am, sir," said Perkins respectfully.

So Marmalade followed Rufus into the back of the horsebox, which was not arranged like an ordinary horsebox, but was very smartly furnished, with club chairs and piles of richly embroidered cushions. Marmalade noticed a small cocktail cabinet in one corner, full of dark brown bottles. Marmalade sat in one of the chairs, and Rufus sprawled elegantly on the cushions. Perkins started the engine up and drove away.

Marmalade was dying to know where they were going and what they were going to do, but Rufus didn't seem inclined to say any more. He just lay on his cushions, thoughtfully pulling dried mud and burrs out of his shaggy coat, and taking occasional swigs from one of the brown bottles. In the end Marmalade couldn't stand it.

"All right, clever," she said. "Where are we going?"

"Place I know," said Rufus. "You'll like it."

"I hope there'll be something to eat," said Marmalade. "I'm starving."

"Oh, I always get plenty to eat there," said Rufus.

"Listen, donkey," said Marmalade. "I don't eat hay, you know. I want proper grub and plenty of it."

"Fancy yourself, don't you?" said Rufus. "If I say you'll be all right, Marmalade Atkins, you'll be all right. I'm going to make you a star tonight, I am."

"Fat chance," said Marmalade.

"You'll see," said Rufus.

Then the horsebox stopped and Perkins came round to open the back door. When Marmalade got out she saw that they were outside a long low building standing on its own on a grassy hill. There was a car park full of big cars and a little neon sign in fancy handwriting saying

EL POKO NIGHTCLUB AND RESTAURANT
LIVE SHOW TONIGHT

"Come on, Atkins," said Rufus. "Let's get among 'em."

"We can't go in a place like this!" said Marmalade. "They'll throw us out!"

"Like to see 'em try," said Rufus.

As they approached the entrance, a very big man in evening dress stepped into their path. He had a face like a large joint of beef and he did not seem to be in a very good mood.

"Just a minute, John," he said to Rufus. "Where d'you think you're going?"

"In here, for a bit of fun," said Rufus.

"No chance, John," said the man. "On your way."

"You must be new here," said Rufus. "My name's Rufus, not John. Kindly step aside. Me and Marmalade Atkins are getting cold."

"More than me job's worth, John," said the man. "No jeans, all pets on leads. Evening dress tonight. On your bike, the pair of you. El Poko, this is, not the Sally Army."

Marmalade suddenly felt herself getting very angry. "Don't you talk to my donkey like that," she said. "These are my best jeans, you know. And look at his bow tie. He looks a lot nicer than you do. You look like a dog's breakfast!"

"Right," said the meat-faced man. He put his huge hand against Rufus's chest and gave him a push. This was rather silly of him, because Rufus didn't move an inch. The meat-faced man began to look rather worried as he realised he had bitten off more than he could chew.

Rufus put his nose against the meat-faced man's chest and gave him a gentle nudge. The meat-faced man staggered back a couple of paces into the doorway.

"Watch it," he said, in a voice that had gone rather high and weak.

Rufus gave him another nudge, just a little bit harder, and the meat-faced man flew backwards through the doorway and into the restaurant, where he sat down rather suddenly on the thick purple carpet.

"Here," said the meat-faced man. "I don't want no violence."

"Fair enough, John," said Rufus, and Rufus and Marmalade Atkins entered El Poko Nightclub and Restaurant.

Marmalade, expecting more trouble, glared around her, trying to look a lot braver than she felt. El Poko Nightclub and Restaurant was full of little tables with candles and flowers on them and fat rich-looking ladies and gentlemen eating huge platefuls of meat and vegetables and drinking huge bottles of posh-looking wine. They all looked up as Marmalade and Rufus came in and there was a short and deathly silence.

Then, to Marmalade's amazement, a great cheer went up. The fat ladies and gentlemen were jumping up from their tables and shouting: "It's Rufus! Good old Rufus! Sock it to 'em Rufus!" Rufus acknowledged these frenzied greetings with a casual wave of his hoof, and led the way to a table in the corner, stepping over the meat-faced man, who slunk away snarling.

Marmalade noticed that the table had an extra

large bunch of flowers on it, and a very strong-looking old fashioned oak bench behind it. Rufus sat down on the bench, and Marmalade sat opposite him. All the fat ladies and gentlemen were still staring at them, as well they might, thought Marmalade. But she stared back as haughtily as she could.

"Interestin' flowers," said Rufus, and before Marmalade could do anything about it, he leant over, seized the whole bunch in his teeth, and ate them. Marmalade stared in horror at her diabolical old donkey as he sat there in his bow tie, his muddy hooves on the dazzling white tablecloth, with last shreds of orchid and carnation dangling colourfully from the corner of his mouth. The fat ladies and gentlemen were laughing fit to bust (in fact one of the fat gentlemen did bust his trousers and had to rush out to the cloakroom) and out of the corner of her eye Marmalade saw the manager rushing over to their table.

Oh, blimey, thought Marmalade.

But Rufus didn't turn one dirty ginger hair.

"Very tasty," he said to the manager.

The manager swallowed.

"I am very happy, sir," he said. Marmalade thought he looked more nervous than happy, but so long as he wasn't yanking Rufus and Marmalade out of their seats and booting them out the back door, she wasn't going to argue the toss. "You like to order now, sir?" said the manager. "We got a very nice stuffed peperonies?"

"Can't get on with mucked about foreign

rubbish," said Rufus. "No hard feelings. I'll just have a double chef's salad, two pound of leeks, lightly sweated in butter, the Carrot Special, twice, a couple of marrows, bag of oats and a few apples. I can't eat much when I'm working."

"Yes sir," said the manager, scribbling fast. "Tossed in the salad bowl with dressing?"

"No, in the bag," said Rufus.

"And for madame?" said the manager.

"Sausage and chips," said Marmalade Atkins. It seemed a bit of an anti-climax after Rufus's order.

"Thank you, madame," said the manager. "A double portion?"

"Treble," said Marmalade grandly. The manager bowed low and she felt much better.

"On the plate, with a knife and fork, and two sorts of sauce," she added. The manager bowed so low he looked as if he was thinking of crawling under the table for a lie down.

When the food came, the conversation stopped for a time. Neither Marmalade nor Rufus believed in a lot of chat when there was food about. In any case, Rufus would have found it rather difficult, because his food was in a huge nosebag embroidered with his name in sequins on velvet, and it was so heavy and full that it took two big waitresses to hoist it over his ears. They ate for a long time, and Marmalade began to feel very satisfied and sleepy. She swallowed the last chip and laid down her knife and fork just as the waitresses were unhooking Rufus's nosebag.

"That was great," she said. "Are we going home now?"

"No," said Rufus. "This is where the fun really starts," and he wiped his chops on the tablecloth and put on a straw hat with a striped ribbon.

"Bit later on," he said, "you and me are going to do a song on that there stage."

For the first time Marmalade noticed a small stage at the side of the restaurant.

"Ha ha," she said. "If you think I'm going to get up on there in front of all these people and sing a song with a donkey in a straw hat you've got another think coming."

"Money's good," said Rufus. "And they'll swallow anything will this lot."

Marmalade wanted to ask him what on earth he was talking about when suddenly the lights went down.

"Got to go now," said Rufus, and suddenly Marmalade was sitting by herself at the table in the dark, and a lot of bright lights were shining on the stage.

The manager came on to the middle of the stage and talked into a microphone.

"Ladies and gentlemen," he said.

"Get off," shouted the ladies and gentlemen.

"Without further ado," said the manager, "I'll call on the beast you've been waiting for . . . the diabolical donkey . . . your friend and my friend . . . GOOD-TIME RUFUS!"

The band started to play, and before Marmalade had time to wonder whether she was dreaming, there was Rufus on the stage, straw hat tipped over one ear, strutting about as the audience cheered and threw flowers in the air, and while the cheering was still at its height, he began to sing:

"They call me Good-Time Rufus, cos a good time is what I always get,
Yes, I'm Good-Time Rufus, all the ladies' favourite pet,
If I don't like your style you get a poke in the tum
And Good-Time Rufus gonna kick you in the daisies,
Yes I'm Good-Time Rufus and I never had a bad time yet!"

Tum does not rhyme with daisies, thought Marmalade to herself, but apart from that it was a pretty good song. And there was no doubt that the audience loved it. As Rufus tipped off his straw hat with his left forefoot, caught it on his right and twirled it round, the men were cheering and the ladies were screaming and fainting all over the place. Even the meat-faced man was clapping sulkily. Marmalade called for a dandelion and burdock and settled down to enjoy the show.

It was quite a varied show. Rufus sang a number of songs, including jolly up-tempo numbers like "I'm Your Big Cabbage and Oats Man", and sentimental ditties (Marmalade thought "Ass Time Goes By" was downright soppy but she had to admit that his performance of "You'll Never

Trot Alone" brought a little lump to her throat).

In between the songs he told donkey jokes (Hear about the donkey who tried tap dancing? Fell in the bath), insulted members of the audience (they seemed to love it), tried a bit of roller skating (which was not quite so successful as he fell off the stage twice and squashed a whole party of town clerks and their wives, but they seemed to regard it as quite an honour), and finished up with some donkey imitations, which he said were the most difficult imitations there were. These were greeted with the loudest applause of all. The audience were clearly a lot of mad idiots, thought Marmalade.

Then suddenly a bright light was shining in her eyes, and all the people had turned round to look at her, and up on the stage that dreadful power-drunk donkey was *talking* about her and *pointing* at her.

"Let's have a big hand" he was saying "for Dangerous Marmalade Atkins!"

All the ladies and gentlemen clapped and cheered.

"I'm not going up there," said Marmalade.

"Oh yes you are," said Rufus.

"Oh no I'm not," said Marmalade.

"Oh yes she is," shouted the audience like sheep at a pantomime.

It was like a bad dream. I'm going to put a stop to these daft capers, thought Marmalade, and stamped up on to the stage.

But when she got there in the bright lights and

the heat, she found that she liked the feeling of standing next to her sweaty old donkey hearing the cheers of the crowd. The applause died down, the band started playing again, and Marmalade found that her brain was mysteriously filling up with the words of a song, as if someone had made a hole in the top of her head and poured them in with a jug. And this is how it went:

Rufus: Who wants to be a little dear?
Marmalade: I don't!
Rufus: Who wants curly ringlets down to here?
Marmalade: I don't!
Rufus: Who goes to parties in a white chiffon dress?
Marmalade: I never wear a dress!
               I like to look a mess!
Rufus: Who always does what Mummy says?
Marmalade: I don't!
Rufus: Who loves her dolly and her Ted?
Marmalade: *I* don't!
Rufus: Who wants to be a beauty queen too?
Marmalade: Well I don't
Rufus: And I don't
Marmalade and Rufus: Cos all we want
               Is to stamp and shout
               And put ourselves
               about!
               Marmalade and
               Rufus!
                 RAH RAH RAH!

On a sudden impulse, Marmalade jumped on to
Rufus's back, and he hurled himself off the stage
and began doing his hee-haw zigzags in and out
amongst the tables. Every time a table went over
the ladies and gentlemen laughed and cheered
and clapped. They need their heads seeing to,
thought Marmalade grimly as she clung on for
dear life to Rufus's bow tie. The terrified features
of the meat-faced man loomed up directly ahead
of them.

"Out of the way, meat-face!" shrieked

Marmalade, and the fear-crazed bouncer dived straight into a tank of live trout as Rufus wheeled sharply to the right and galloped through the emergency exit, followed by the crowd of fans. To her relief Marmalade saw that the horsebox was standing outside with Perkins holding the door open. Rufus galloped straight in with Marmalade still on his back, and in a moment Perkins had the door shut and they were speeding away from El Poko Nightclub and Restaurant.

It seemed amazingly quiet in the back, after the mad scenes they had just been through. Marmalade lay on the cushions and Rufus sat on the chair. He seemed his usual dozy self again. After a bit, he cleared his throat.

"Not a bad night," said Rufus, "all things considered."

Marmalade thought that was putting it mildly.

"Do you carry on like that," she said, "every time you go to the El Poko?"

"More or less," said Rufus. "Seems to go down all right."

"The bit that got me," said Marmalade, "was the donkey imitations. I don't know how you have the nerve."

"Ah," said Rufus. "See, what they think is, I'm a human being dressed up in a donkey suit."

"They must be barmy," said Marmalade.

"Well," said Rufus, "you can fool some of the people all of the time, and all of the people some of the time. I reckon these are the people you can fool all of the time."

Marmalade found this a bit hard to follow, and the cushions were deliciously comfortable.

"Mind you," said Rufus. "I've always found you can fool most of the people most of the time. Or to put it another way..."

But Marmalade had gone to sleep.

When she woke up in the morning she thought about the weird events of the night. Absolutely ridiculous. This time it just had to be a dream. But no. She was still wearing her best jeans, she could still taste sausages and dandelion and burdock, and on the pillow by her head was a very grubby crumpled envelope with "M. Atkins" written on it in the messiest handwriting Marmalade had ever seen. Inside were fifteen greasy pound notes and a little note in the same disgusting scrawl:

Yor share of the takins. Put it on a hoss.

G.T.R.

Marmalade Atkins
and the Pyjama Plan

Marmalade Atkins sat opposite her mother at the breakfast table. Her mother was watching her with grave suspicion. Marmalade was not whistling through her teeth. She was not kicking her legs against her chair. She was not scratching her head. She was not balancing her cup on the knob of the teapot. She was sitting very quietly with her hands folded in her lap, like a good girl, and as Mrs Atkins knew Marmalade was an extremely bad girl, she was worried, and her nerves were fraying at the edges like a pair of old jeans.

Marmalade was thinking. She was thinking about the message from G.T.R. The question was: how do you put money on a horse? Marmalade had a seen a lot of things put on horses: saddles, bridles, rosettes, and that sort of thing. She had even (I am sorry to report) put some unusual things on horses herself, such as jam, chickens, her mother's best hat, half a bottle of perfume (when Torchy had been rolling in cow manure) but she did not know how to put money on a horse, nor did she see the point of it.

"Mum," she said. "Can I ask you a question?"

Marmalade's mother stared at her in astonishment. Had her little girl reformed? Was she going to be a good girl now? Had the last ten years been just a bad dream? She decided to test it out.

"I should prefer you to call me Mother, Marmalade."

"Suit yourself, cock," said Marmalade.

Marmalade's mother sighed, and promised herself a new crocodile skin handbag just as soon as she could get on the telephone to Harrods. Perhaps they might even have a whole crocodile, a small but savage one, who would obey Mrs Atkins's every command. Mrs Atkins would buy it a smart leather collar studded with rhinestones, and a silver chain, and it would menace cheeky little girls who called their mothers "Mum" and "Cock" and smashed sofas in the night. It was a lovely thought, but it was not to be. Marmalade's mother sighed again, and said between closed teeth:

"Ask your question, Marmalade."

"How d'you put money on a horse?" said Marmalade.

"I see," said her mother. "You want to branch out. Insulting people and destroying furniture is no longer enough for you, is it? You want to gamble my money away, do you?"

"Got me own money cock, I mean Mothah," said Marmalade. "I just want to know how to do it. Please tell me Mothah. You know such a lot."

Marmalade's mother imagined her little crocodile with its paws on Marmalade's chest, showing all its sharp little teeth and growling musically as Marmalade promised to be a good girl for ever and ever.

"People," said Marmalade's mother, "with more money than sense put money on horses. They go to a horse race, they decide which horse they think is going to win the race, and they give their money to people with even more money and very much more sense, called bookies. If the horse wins the race, the silly people get their money back, and some of the bookie's money as well."

"I see," said Marmalade. "That sounds OK to me."

"It is not OK, however," said her mother. "Because nearly always the silly people pick the wrong horse, and the bookie keeps all their money, and goes home laughing in his Rolls Royce to his country mansion."

"Ah, I see," said Marmalade. "But when I put my money on a horse, it'll win."

"That's what all the silly people say," said Marmalade's mother, wondering whether her crocodile would need a room of its own, or whether she could keep it in the second bathroom.

"In any case," she went on, "you have no money of your own to bet with, and I am certainly not going to give you any. Why can't you play with dolls and go to Brownies, like other girls?"

"Been expelled from the Brownies, haven't I?" said Marmalade. "Wasn't my fault."

"Oh, yes," said her mother, remembering the incident of Brown Owl and the exploding cigars. Perhaps a private tutor would be the thing for her daughter. Mrs Atkins remembered an all-in wrestler she had seen on television one Sunday afternoon: Slopoganga the Witch-Doctor, he was called. He looked the sort of man who could cope with her daughter, if Harrods proved to be out of crocodiles. Filled with new hope, she went upstairs to make some telephone calls, and Marmalade went outside to see the animals.

In the middle of the night Marmalade woke up again. She was getting used to this now, and she pulled her jeans on quickly and went downstairs.

"Where are we going then?" she said.

Rufus looked up.

"Not going out tonight," he said. "Too much work to do."

He was sitting at her father's desk with a green eye shade on, dropping mud and burrs on a lot of newspapers and books as he bent his shaggy head over them and screwed up his eyes.

"What work's that then?" said Marmalade.

"Horse work," said Rufus. "Got to find ourselves a good little race meeting."

"To get our money on a horse?"

"That's it, Marmalade," said Rufus.

"Uttoxeter, Warwick, Wincanton...can't afford to go down there for a bit. Real vicious lot of donkeys they got down Wincanton..."

Marmalade sat and watched him as he muttered and grumbled to himself, his front hooves scoring long grooves in Mr Atkin's walnut desk-top.

"Ah, now," he said. "Here's a funny one. Not

far to go either. Professional *and* amateur. How d'you fancy a bit of jockeying?"

"What in?" said Marmalade.

"Kenilworth Jubilee Midnight Steeplechase. Saturday. Novelty Pyjama Race."

"What'll I ride?" said Marmalade.

"Gypsy, course," said Rufus. "He's a lazy young beggar but he's quick enough when he's got

his rats up. Here, look at this. Prizes presented by Buster Creighton. Now that's a turn up for the book. Been after him for years."

"Now look," said Marmalade. "You're not going to rough him up, are you?"

"No, no," said Rufus shiftily. "Just have a bit of a chat with him. Get his autograph and that."

"Novelty Pyjama Race, eh?" said Marmalade.

"Aye, that's the only snag I can see," said Rufus. "Gypsy hasn't got no pyjamas. Think you could fix him a pair?"

Marmalade worked hard all that week on Gypsy's pyjamas. She was not very good at sewing, which was not really her fault, as she had been banned from needlework at school after only two lessons, when all she had done was to sew Sister Purification to the altar-cloth, and carelessly leave a few needles in Sister Conception's armchair. So it took her a long time to turn all four pairs of her father's striped pyjamas into one big pair for Gypsy. But in the end it was done, and Gypsy stood very patiently to be fitted. The sleeves and legs were too short of course, and there was rather a wide gap of glossy brown belly between the tops and the bottoms, but the hole for his tail was very fetching, and after Rufus and Torchy had had a good tug of war with Marmalade's Brownie Bobble-Hat, and stretched it to something like six times its original size, it made a charming nightcap, which waggled cheekily every time Gypsy moved his ears.

Gypsy was very proud of his pyjamas, and spent a long time walking up and down the side of the stream in them, trying to catch flattering reflections of himself, but Rufus was merciless, and gave him the hee-haw zigzag three times a day to build up his speed.

On Friday night Marmalade's father came home after a hard week with the Arabs, and made rather a silly fuss over some scratches on his desk (Camels, said Marmalade) and was puzzled to find that there were no pyjamas for him to put on. In the end he was forced to go to bed in a burnous that a grateful Arab had given him, which made Marmalade's mother laugh a great deal in a scornful sort of way. Marmalade lay happily in bed listening to her parents shouting and throwing small ornaments at each other. This time tomorrow night, she said to herself, me and Rufus and Gypsy will be there with Buster Creighton and all the big nobs of the racing world at the Kenilworth Jubilee Midnight Steeplechase!

Marmalade, Rufus, and the Midnight Steeplechase

Marmalade stood under a huge dark tree in the Kenilworth Abbey Fields. It was a cold night, but she had the smooth glossy steadily breathing warmth of Gypsy on one side of her, and Rufus's shaggy burr-encrusted coat on the other. She was eating a Monster Hot Dog, and she was feeling great.

She had been to the Abbey Fields before, but never at night. Everything looked so different that when Perkins drove the extra-large horsebox into the car park, she thought he'd come to the wrong place. The great trees loomed like monsters, with flares and floodlights making crazy shadows in the branches above, and everywhere there were horseboxes, crowds, horses of all shapes and sizes, fat men with checked suits and big leather bags full of pound notes and betting tickets, a silver band, hot dog and candyfloss stalls, and a tent which sold beer, for the men to march into and stagger out of.

Rufus had instructed her to stay quietly with Gypsy under the tree while he went about his business. He didn't tell her what his business was, but it seemed to involve a lot of quiet talking and arguing with some of the men in checked suits, and some hurried consultations with one or two of the horses in the early races.

The early races had all been for classy horses, the sort of horses that went to real race-meetings and point-to-points. Three of them had jockeys in real racing silks, bad-tempered hungry-looking little men who carried whips and used them on their horses, and these three nasty little men had won all the first three races between them. Marmalade had watched intently, trying to pick up tips. The thing to do seemed to be to get into the lead right at the start, then get in the path of the other horses. A tall, snooty-looking hunter called Nigel's Folly had done this in the second race, and none of the others had been able to get past him.

"Right awkward swine, that Nigel's Folly," said Rufus. "Still, he won't be in the pyjama race, he's too posh for that."

Marmalade felt glad. Even though she knew she was the best and most ruthless rider in the world, and Gypsy the fastest horse in Warwickshire, she also knew in another part of her mind that Nigel's Folly looked about twice the size of Gypsy, and though she and Gypsy had smashed up a few gymkhanas and been barred from three local showjumping events, neither of them had actually been in a horse race before, let alone a Midnight Steeplechase.

The loudspeaker boomed:

"Horse and riders to the paddock please, for the Novelty Pyjama Steeplechase. Horses entered: Arthritis, Galloping Consumption, Effervescence, Mad Gypsy Atkins, Harbottle's Revenge . . .

"Quick, Marmalade, get him in his 'jamas," said Rufus, and they started to dress Gypsy, who was trembling with pride and excitement.

"... Hair of the Dog, Housemaid's Knee, Catfish," boomed on the loudspeaker, "Educated Arbuckle, Hole in One, and a late entry ... Nigel's Folly."

"Blight and mildew," said Rufus. "We been double-crossed. Quick, over to the paddock."

When they got to the paddock most of the other horses were parading sedately round the ring, surrounded by a quiet crowd who stared at their legs trying to decide which would go fastest. Marmalade scrambled up, nudged Gypsy in the pyjama buttons, and joined the parade. To her surprise and rage a great roar of laughter went up from the crowd. It took her a moment or two to realise what they were laughing at. Rufus had got it wrong. It was the *riders* that were supposed to be in pyjamas, not the horses.

Marmalade tried to rise above it all, but she could feel her face getting redder and redder as Gypsy plodded round the ring, the bobble on his Brownie hat bouncing this way and that. Nasty little boys and girls were shouting and pointing, nasty fat men in pork pie hats were calling out witty remarks, and up on the judges' stand, a big burly man was falling about laughing.

"Buster Creighton," said Rufus. "He's got it coming to him, he has."

"You fool, Rufus!" hissed Marmalade. "It's all your fault."

"Never an ill wind," said Rufus. "Look at the bookies' boards."

Marmalade looked across. All the bookies were furiously rubbing out figures and writing in new ones. Most of the writing had to do with Nigel's Folly and Mad Gypsy Atkins. Opposite Nigel's Folly they were writing up EVENS and opposite Mad Gypsy Atkins they were writing 20–1.

"Is that good?" said Marmalade. "Will we get a lot of money if we win?"

"*If* we win," said Rufus grimly. "I better do something about that now."

Marmalade watched him trot up alongside Nigel's Folly. He looked tiny beside the huge steeplechaser. People round the ropes laughed and said "Ahhh" as they saw the little donkey raising his head, as if he were talking to the jockey. Marmalade didn't laugh because she could hear what he was saying.

"Listen, Vic," Rufus said out of the side of his mouth to the nasty little man. "It ain't your night tonight. All the big money's on the Mad Gypsy. You got to take a dive at the third fence."

Vicious Vic Halibut (this was the nasty little man's name) made no reply except to lean over and hit Rufus on the backside with his whip. Now he's for it, thought Marmalade, but Rufus merely shook his head and trotted on.

"All right, Vic," he said. "Don't say we didn't warn you."

"Get that donkey out of here," snarled Vicious Vic Halibut, and the loudspeaker boomed:

"All donkeys to leave the paddock immediately please!"

Rufus dodged a steward and came trotting back to Marmalade. "Quick, give us your money," he said. "I better get it on each way."

Marmalade gave him the fifteen pounds, and he galumphed over the ropes and began an argument with the biggest of the bookies. In less than a minute he was back, with two stewards vainly trying to drag him out.

"Cor, what a caper," he said breathlessly. "Bookie says he don't bet with donkeys or Welshmen. You'll have to get the money on yourself. Get a move on, I'll look after old Gypsy."

Marmalade leapt off and ran over to the bookie.

"Hello little girl," said the bookie, his huge red nose gleaming in the lamplight like a Christmas Tree decoration. "Want a little bet do you?"

"Yes I do," said Marmalade.

"Ten pee each way on Nigel's Folly, is it?" said the bookie.

"Not likely," said Marmalade haughtily. "Fifteen pounds on Mad Gypsy Atkins."

The bookie stared in amazement at her handful of notes. It was the biggest bet he had taken all night.

"On the nose?" he said.

"Of course on the nose," said Marmalade, wondering what on the nose meant.

"Know something, do you?" said the bookie, as

if he were anxious but trying not to sound like it.

"Course I do," said Marmalade. "I know who's going to win."

The bookie went pale, and handed her a ticket.

"Three hundred to fifteen the Mad Gypsy," he said.

The loudspeaker boomed:

"Runners and riders to the starting line."

Marmalade pocketed the ticket and ran to the start, where the horses were lined up snorting and snuffling and the riders were glaring grimly at each other.

"Get it on all right?" said Rufus, as she climbed back on Gypsy.

"Yes. On the nose," said Marmalade, proud of knowing the right words.

"Oh blimey," said Rufus. "That means we've got to win."

"Huh!" said Marmalade. "Me and Gypsy have got to win, not you, Mister Clever Rufus, and a fine mess you've got us into!"

The loudspeaker boomed:

"All donkeys off the starting line *please*! Will that scruffy ginger donkey's owner please remove him at once!"

"I'm me own donkey," grumbled Rufus. "All right, all right, I'm going."

He shuffled away into the darkness behind the horses, and Marmalade couldn't see him any more. It was all up to her and Gypsy now, and it didn't look too promising. She found herself next in line to Nigel's Folly, and Vicious Vic Halibut sneered down at her from what seemed like a very great height.

"Little girls up past their bedtimes, ponies in pyjamas," said Vicious Vic. "Didn't ought to be allowed. You better keep out of the way, midget."

"Don't worry, Fishface," said Marmalade. "You won't see our tail for dust."

Vicious Vic laughed a nasty laugh, and barged Nigel's Folly into Gypsy's side. Gypsy looked up mildly, and nuzzled his pyjama-ed flank against the steeplechaser's bridle. That was the trouble with Gypsy. He liked everyone, and he never took offence. He also looked as if he was just ready to be tucked up in bed and told a nice story, instead of running a race against some of the fastest horses in Warwickshire.

Buster Creighton came to the edge of the judges' stand with a big flag. When he saw Gypsy he started laughing again, and Marmalade put her tongue out at him. Buster Creighton stopped laughing and raised two fingers at Marmalade.

"That's the Victory sign," she told Gypsy. "Come on, wake up. This is your big moment, you soft horse!"

But Gypsy just waggled his Brownie hat, simply happy to be standing around with a lot of other nice horses in a big field in the middle of the night.

"Oh well," thought Marmalade Atkins. "There goes my fifteen pounds."

Buster Creighton raised the flag slowly above his head. Then, just as he was about to bring it down again, everything started happening. Marmalade heard an irregular pounding of hooves just behind her, then the air was rent with a terrible sound, a sort of cross between a mad trombonist and a hundred creaky gates. Rufus was doing a hee-haw zigzag!

The effect on the horses was electrifying! Harbottle's Revenge tossed his rider straight on to Arthritis, who buckled at the knees and lay down for a long rest. Catfish bucked into the crowd and Hole in One ran into the judges' stand. Nearly all the other horses were bumping into each other, turning round, whinnying in fright, and fleeing in all directions.

But Gypsy was off like a rocket, running dead straight as he always did, with Nigel's Folly hard at his heels.

"Hee-haw," went Rufus, and Gypsy kicked off at the first fence, sending a shower of mud into Vicious Vic Halibut's face. Marmalade clung on grimly, gripping hard with her knees. Gypsy had the Red Mist, and there was nothing to be done but try to stay on his back. Marmalade could see the fences coming towards her through the darkness at terrifying speed, stewards diving to right and left as Mad Gypsy Atkins bore down on them. But he sailed over every fence as if it wasn't there.

After the first six fences, Marmalade risked a look back. She nearly fell off, but managed to see that there were only about four horses left in the race and the only one within twenty yards was

Nigel's Folly, with Vicious Vic Halibut screaming and cursing and whacking him with the whip. Marmalade turned back just in time to see an enormous tree rushing straight at them. Gypsy had gone straight on at the bend! She pulled with all her might on the left hand rein, and Gypsy skidded to a halt, thumping into the treetrunk with the seat of his pyjamas. He stared round wildly, wondering where to run next.

In a frantic rage, Marmalade saw Nigel's Folly

round the bend and and make for the home straight. Effervescence and Housemaid's Knee were not far behind. She wasn't going to win after all.

Then, to her relief, she heard the irregular pounding and the horrible braying again as Rufus rushed up in one final wheezing effort. Gypsy laid his ears back in terror, and hurtled after Nigel's

Folly. He had never suffered two hee-haw zigzags in quick succession before, and there was no stopping him.

Two fences from the finish, Vicious Vic Halibut heard them coming. With a fearful snarl, he leaned over and aimed a blow of his whip at Gypsy's bobble-hat. But Gypsy, his teeth bared in a daft grin, went by so fast that Halibut missed completely, and zoomed off his horse with the force of his own blow. Nigel's Folly looked down at him in the mud, then trotted off to his horsebox. He had never liked Vicious Vic Halibut much anyway.

Gypsy shot over the last fence and crossed the finishing line still going at full speed. Marmalade caught a glimpse of the white and startled faces of the judges going by in a blur, and turned to give Buster Creighton a Victory sign. When she turned round again, there was something big and white coming towards them.

"Oh, no," she said. "Not the beer tent."

Gypsy went into the beer tent at forty miles an hour, and cleared two trestle tables in fine style. Then he banged into the centre pole and the whole tent slowly billowed down over Gypsy, Marmalade Atkins, and sixty-seven terrified boozers, thirty-four of whom were so impressed by the incident that they never went in a beer tent again.

There was a long silence. The crowds outside slowly took their hands away from their eyes in time to see Gypsy slowly emerge from the wreckage, with Marmalade still clinging round his neck. He had lost the bottom half of his pyjamas, and he had a mildly puzzled look on his face, like someone who had just woken from a long and pleasant dream.

Marmalade trotted him up to the bookie's stand.

"Take him away," said the bookie, handing a big bundle of notes across with a shaking hand. "I never want to see him again."

"Fair enough," said Marmalade.

"And from now on," said the bookie, "I don't bet with Welshmen, donkeys, *or* little girls."

Marmalade trotted him over to the judges' stand.

"Take him away," said Buster Creighton, handing over a rather small cup with a shaking hand. "No more midnight steeplechases for me."

"Suit yourself, cock," said Marmalade, giving him another Victory sign. "See you at Olympia, eh?"

Buster Creighton went pale.

The crowds fell back respectfully on either side as Marmalade and Gypsy walked sedately back towards the horsebox. When they got to the horsebox, Gypsy went in and settled down to a nice bag of oats. Marmalade looked round for Rufus. He was nowhere to be seen.

"Where's Rufus, Perkins?" she said.

"Don't know Miss," said Perkins. "Said he had a bit of business."

Marmalade looked back towards the judges' stand in the distance, and saw a burly man trying to push a scruffy ginger donkey off the platform.

"Oh dear," said Marmalade.

The scruffy ginger donkey gave the burly man an affectionate nudge. The burly man staggered. The scruffy ginger donkey gave the burly man another affectionate nudge. Marmalade closed her eyes.

When she opened them, Buster Creighton was lying flat on his back in the mud, and Rufus was standing on his chest.

Marmalade Atkins
and the Sacred Heart

Things went quietly at the farm for a week or two after that. There were no more night conversations, no more outings to El Poko Nightclub and Restaurant, no more Midnight Steeplechases. Rufus fell out with his girlfriend Jenny and made it up again, Torchy rolled in some wet cement that the neighbouring farmer was making a drive with, and got himself a cement overcoat that made him buckle at the knees, Gypsy got the Red Mist one day and ran in a straight line to Nuneaton, stopping for nothing and nobody. This involved several small traffic accidents, a policeman who got such a fright that his hair went white, and rumours of unidentified flying objects all over Warwickshire. Gypsy came back in a police van looking mild and affable, as if it had been some other horse altogether.

One day Marmalade's mother brought a very tall black gentleman to see the farm. She introduced him as Doctor Slopoganga, and said he was a private tutor, who would transform Marmalade Atkins into a respectable young lady in no time at all. Marmalade showed him round. First she persuaded him to have a ride on Gypsy. After he had been pulled out of the duckpond, he was taken to meet the goat, who ate most of his witchdoctor's feathered headdress with great enjoyment, but was very soon sick.

"He liked it really, cock," said Marmalade to Doctor Slopoganga, trying to console him because he looked so sad. "He's just got a rotten digestion, nothing to do with you."

Doctor Slopoganga said nothing; he was trying to remember a powerful curse for little girls and goats that his grandmother had taught him.

Later, Rufus came back from a visit to Jenny. He took to Doctor Slopoganga at once, and gave him a few affectionate nudges. Doctor Slopoganga was used to flying drop kicks and piledrivers, and he stood up to Rufus's nudges remarkably well. It took about six of them before Doctor Slopoganga was lying on his back with Rufus's forefeet on his chest. Doctor Slopoganga tapped three times on Rufus's hoof.

"Submit," said the witchdoctor.

Marmalade's mother came out of the farmhouse.

"It's only his way of showing he likes you," she said, biting her lip. But Doctor Slopoganga was not to be consoled. He got in his car, and drove slowly back to London, counting his blessings. Rolling round the wrestling ring with such as Giant Haystacks and The Mad Axeman was a doddle when you compared it with private tutoring on quiet Warwickshire farms with little girls and their donkeys.

Then, about a week later, Mrs Allgood came back. Marmalade came into the lounge to find her sitting on the sofa in a new and dreadful hat, talking to Marmalade's mother.

"Back again, cock?" said Marmalade.

"Hello, dear," said Mrs Allgood nervously, holding on to her hat with both hands. Her understanding smile was not what it had been. In fact it was a kind of demented grin, as if she hadn't understood anything at all for quite a long time. Some said that working on the computers had done that to her; people who knew better said it was Marmalade.

"Mrs Allgood has brought some good news," said Marmalade's mother uneasily.

"Oh yeah?" said Marmalade suspiciously, advancing a step or two.

"Yes, dear," said Mrs Allgood, trying to remind herself that Marmalade was only a little girl, after all. "The Sisters of the Sacred Heart Convent have been persuaded to take you back again for a trial period!"

"Oh, goody gumdrops," said Marmalade sarcastically. "Why?"

"Well dear," said Mrs Allgood. "They, er, felt, that with Christmas coming, and the spirit of goodwill, and with so much suffering in the world, that it wouldn't be right if they didn't take on their share of suffering too. They're very good like that."

"I'm not going back to that dump," said Marmalade.

"It's that or Borstal," said her mother brutally.

Marmalade thought about it.

"I'll take the Sacred Heart," she said.

Thus it was that Marmalade Atkins found herself once again sitting on the old school bench in a soppy uniform with a lot of wets and softies listening to Sister Purification, who seemed to be in a state of high excitement.

"Girls," said Sister Purification. "Our school has been chosen to present the annual Nativity Play in Coventry Precinct!"

"Ooh!" went all the softies dutifully, the vile Cherith Ponsonby oohing loudest of all.

"Big deal," said Marmalade Atkins. Sister Purification gave her a look of deep hatred, but remembered her vow of patience and suffering and restricted herself to snapping a few pencils.

"Sister Conception will now announce the cast," said Sister Purification.

Sister Conception stepped forward. She was a big burly nun with a moustache. Marmalade liked Sister Conception's moustache; in fact it was the only thing she liked about Sister Conception. Marmalade rather hoped for a moustache when she grew up, but if *she* had one she would wax the ends and twirl it, instead of letting it grow all straggly and uncared for as Sister Conception did.

But it was time for the Reading of the Cast, and all the wets and softies were trembling on the edge of their seats.

"Mary: Cherith Ponsonby." Some of the softies actually clapped, and Cherith Ponsonby sat back smugly.

"Joseph: Oonagh Clodd."

Marmalade gave a derisive guffaw and Sister Conception went on quickly:
"Shepherds: Teresa Murphy, Teresa Pratt, Teresa Sullivan.

Kings: Mary O'Malley, Mary McSharry, and Mary Cohen.

Angels: Eileen Rogan, Eileen Hogan, Eileen Gogan . . ."

"Hang on a bit, cock," said Marmalade Atkins. "What about me? I want to be the one who kills all the boys."

"Herod is not in this play, Marmalade Atkins," said Sister Purification with some satisfaction.

"Why not?" said Marmalade. "He's the best character in the whole story, and I've got this Arab sword I could use to kill 'em with."

"There is to be *no Herod*," said Sister Purification.

"All right then, I want to be a king," said Marmalade.

"No!"

"What am I going to be then?" said Marmalade.

"You do not deserve a part at all, as you are such a wicked and evil little girl," said Sister Purification. "However, as it is Christmas, we have decided to give you a chance. You are to be . . . the Innkeeper!"

She made it sound like something very special, but Marmalade was not easily fooled.

What does he do?" she said.

"He is the one who actually tells Mary and

Joseph that there is *no room* at the *inn*!"

"Is that all?" said Marmalade. "Pathetic!"

"It is a very important part and you are a wicked and ungrateful little girl."

"Look," said Marmalade. "Innkeepers do a lot more than that. Couldn't he throw a few drunks out or something? Look, I know, a lot of Arabs turn up at the inn on their camels and start smashing up sofas. The innkeeper takes them all on. There's this enormous fight, and the innkeeper wins, but his front room's completely destroyed. No room at the inn. Get it?"

With a strangled roar, Sister Purification yanked a leg off the table and strode down the aisle. But Sister Conception laid a restraining hand on her.

"Not on her first day back, Sister Purification," she said.

Sister Purification retired muttering to a corner.

"The only thing, girls," said Sister Conception, "is that we need a donkey, and we haven't been able to get hold of one."

Marmalade Atkins smiled.

"I've got a donkey," she said.

Marmalade, Rufus
and the Nativity Play

It was the last Saturday before Christmas and Coventry Shopping Precinct was packed with people, all full of the Christmas spirit, all fighting each other to get to the counters of toy shops, men crowding into the pubs to perform disappearing tricks behind clouds of smoke and huge mugs of dark brown beer, and women struggling along with pushchairs and parcels, slapping the goose-pimpled legs of their children to give them something to cry about.

Marmalade Atkins watched the whole scene with a curled lip of disdain as she waited outside her cardboard inn for the weary travellers to make their way down from the Cathedral. The past weeks had been terrible. All the little angels poncing about with their harps and wings, all the little shepherds waving their beribboned crooks about, and vile Cherith Ponsonby strutting about looking radiantly beautiful in her Virgin Mary kit, throwing her weight about and generally behaving like a cross between Snow White and the lady who read the news on the television.

And to put the tin lid on it, Rufus, the so-called Diabolical Donkey, had behaved perfectly all through rehearsals. He had walked when they said walk, he had stopped when they said stop, he had let them put haloes on him, he had lain down by the papier maché cow and the cardboard horse and treated them like old mates, instead of kicking them to smithereens. Not once had he nudged Sister Purification down and stood on her chest, not once had he chewed Sister Conception's beads off. No, he had been good. And that was bad.

And now here they all came down the long slope from the Cathedral, with the Sacred Heart Recorder and Percussion Band wailing and clanking and tinkling and thumping along in front of them. The mothers stopped slapping their children's legs and the children stopped howling, and the fathers came to the doorways of the pubs and stood grinning dopily with beer glasses in their hands, everyone in Coventry suddenly feeling the warm tender Christmas spirit as they gazed at the sweet little donkey with the beautiful little girl on his back, plodding quietly towards the very centre of the Precinct where Marmalade the innkeeper stood waiting. It was all too sickening for words.

The band stopped playing and came to a halt, and all the little recorder players stood in a ring smiling sweetly and shaking the spittle out of their recorders. Rufus, the traitor, stood as still as a statue, as if there was nothing in the world he wanted except to be the good little Christmas donkey and have Cherith Ponsonby on his back.

Oonagh Clodd, who was looking rather nervous, stepped forward.

"Good evening," she said. "Is there any room

at the inn? My wife and I have travelled many miles, and she is weary and great with child. Have you a bed for us?"

All eyes turned to Marmalade Atkins.

"Yeah, come on in!" she shouted. "Plenty of room at the inn, cock! Bring the donkey and all, the drinks are on me!"

There was a stunned silence. Then Cherith Ponsonby forgot herself.

"Marmalade Atkins," she said in a clear piercing voice, "you are a mean pig!"

And she got off Rufus's back and kicked him smartly in the leg.

Rufus turned his head round slowly to look at her. He looked as if he was waking from a long dream. Then he pawed the ground with his left forefoot and a wild look came into his eyes. He flung his head back and let loose an enormous hee-haw that echoed round the Precinct and shook the windows of Woolworth's and the British Home Stores. Then he started dancing up and down on all four feet, whirling round in circles and hee-hawing in all directions.

People began to laugh and shout and flock in from all around to look at the crazy Christmas donkey, and this seemed to exhilarate Rufus. He stood up on his hind legs, let loose another ear-splitting howl, then charged the cardboard inn. The papier maché cow was catapulted into the middle of the recorder band, and the cardboard horse collapsed sideways with a soft sigh, completely burying the vile Cherith Ponsonby and

muffling her enraged shrieks. Marmalade just had
time to grab hold of Rufus's bridle and swing
herself on to his scruffy old back before he crashed
through the back wall of the inn to freedom.

There had never been a hee-haw zigzag in
Coventry Precinct before, and at first, as Rufus
hurtled in and out of the arches hee-hawing gaily,
they flocked out of the shops to enjoy the show,
laughing and cheering and trying to pat him as he
went by. But when they saw what he did to the
Bulkington Silver Band, they changed their minds,
and in no time at all the Precinct was a mass of
scurrying men women and children flocking back
inside the shops, pubs and cafes to cower behind
the doors, peeping out in terrified bewilderment as
Rufus harried the last stragglers to their bolt-
holes.

Soon the Precinct was empty and deserted; it looked more like a wet Monday night than the last Saturday before Christmas, but still Rufus zigzagged and hee-hawed as if daring the whole of Coventry to come out and face him. By now he was an alarming sight, festooned with tinsel and holly that he had swept off the shop fronts, clattering and jangling through the bent instruments and scraps of uniform that were all that was left of the Bulkington Silver Band. From time to time, little groups of brave policemen edged nervously out of doorways and tried to grab him, but every time he scattered them and sent them fleeing for safety.

Marmalade could see nothing but a mad blur of Marks and Woolworth's, British Home Spencer's, whimpering Father Christmases and upside-down policemen, and then she became aware that they had changed direction and were pounding uphill towards the Leofric Hotel.

The Leofric Hotel is a very posh hotel, some say the poshest hotel in Coventry. In the week before Christmas they were booked solid, putting on great gluttonous banquets for busloads of big businessmen, jangling mobs of mayors and aldermen in their chains, and gangs of bishops in ther best purple robes boring each other to screaming point about the True Meaning of Christmas. The manager of the Leofric Hotel was not ready to welcome a maddened donkey bursting through the entrance with a savage small girl clinging desperately to his ears, and he barely had time to step forward and say: "Have you a reservation, madam?" before Rufus had thundered past him and charged up the main staircase and on through the glass doors into the banqueting hall.

By a coincidence, the banqueting hall on that Saturday was full of extremely rich Arabs eating a huge banquet which had been arranged for them by Marmalade's father. They had had a lovely meal of turkey and sheep's eyes, couscous and sprouts, washed down with raki and champagne and Brew XI, and they were just in the mood for a cabaret.

"By the Beard of the Prophet!" they chorused as one man. "Eez Good-Time Rufus!"

Rufus skidded to a halt, hee-hawed, gave them two quick choruses of "Good-Time Rufus," then bucked Marmalade Atkins neatly off into a huge tureen of couscous, and disappeared down the back stairs.

The Arabs thought it was terrific, and the air rained with jewels and gold.

Marmalade climbed slowly out of the tureen of couscous, and found herself staring straight into the face of her father.

"Just passing through, cock," she said, rather shakily.

Her father stared at her in a puzzled sort of way.

"Hold on a minute, little girl," he said. "Haven't I met you somewhere before?"

"Can't wait," said Marmalade. "Got to find Rufus."

She ran down the back stairs. There were chambermaids peeping out of cupboards, a pile of bishops struggling feebly at the bottom of the stairs, but no Rufus anywhere. She looked in the restaurants, the bedrooms, the kitchens. Nothing. Outside she could hear the wailing of police sirens, fire engines, and ambulances. They were coming to get her and Rufus, but where was he? Were they to be captured redhanded in the Leofric?

Suddenly she noticed another set of stairs going down to the basement. She dodged a couple of burly porters and ran down them. At the bottom was a small brown door, and she burst through that to find herself in a tiny peaceful little bar with brown panelling and pictures of horses and donkeys on the wall. A little old man stood behind the counter similing peacefully.

"Have you seen a—" gasped Marmalade, and the little old man pointed to the corner seat.

And there he was, sitting calmly by himself with a pint of old ale in front of him, and a small dandelion and burdock in front of the seat next to him. Marmalade stood and watched as he drained his old ale in one big gulp and wiped the froth off his damp and scruffy chops.

"Needed that," said Rufus. "Where you been then? I been waiting ages for you."

Marmalade sat down by him and took a drink of dandelion and burdock.

"I s'pose you realise," said Marmalade, "we've gone too far this time."

"Never," said Rufus.

"They've got the whole police force out there," said Marmalade. "They've come for us. I'll get expelled again, and they'll cart you off to the donkey's reformatory."

"Ha," said Rufus. "If they catch us."

"Oh, be reasonable, donkey," said Marmalade. "They're bound to catch us, they'll come round the farm if they don't get us here."

"Ha," said Rufus. "Not going home."

"Eh?" said Marmalade.

"Come on," said Rufus. "We'll be giving old Perkins the abdabs, hanging round here."

"On the slate," he told the little old man behind the bar. The little old man gave a hollow laugh, as if he had heard all that before, and Marmalade and Rufus went out through a little door like a stable door in the corner.

There outside in an alleyway stood the familiar grey horsebox with Perkins at the salute.

"Where to, sir?" said Perkins.

"Follow the signs to the M1," said Rufus, and nudged Marmalade inside.

The doors were closed, the engine started, and the horsebox rumbled off down the little alleyway, as more and more police vans arrived at the front to begin the Great Siege of the Leofric Hotel (which lasted three days and didn't capture a sausage).

Marmalade sat in the club chair and Rufus lolled on the cushions, drinking from a brown bottle.

"M1?" said Marmalade. "Where are we going?"

"London for a start," said Rufus. "We got too big for Warwickshire to hold us, Marmalade Atkins. Me and you . . ." he paused for a final swig ". . . are ready for the Big Time."